D0006772

Billy Beaver

Dave and Pat Sargent are longtime residents of Prairie Grove, Arkansas. Dave, a fourth-generation dairy farmer, began writing in early December of 1990, and Pat, a former teacher, began writing in the fourth grade. They enjoy the outdoors and have a real love for animals.

Billy Beaver

Animal Pride Series
Book 2

By

Dave and Pat Sargent

Beyond The End
By
Sue Rogers

Illustrated by
Jeane Lirley Huff

Ozark Publishing, Inc.
P.O. Box 228
Prairie Grove, AR 72753

Cataloging-in-Publication Data

Sargent, Dave, 1941-
Billy Beaver / by Dave and Pat Sargent ; illustrated by Jeane Lirley Huff.. —Prairie Grove, AR : Ozark Publishing, ©2003.
ix, 36 p. : col. ill. ; 21 cm. (Animal pride series ; 2)
"A new beginning"—Cover.
SUMMARY: When Billy is told to leave home, he finds himself alone in the woods. Scared but brave, Billy struggles to conquer his fears. Includes facts about the physical characteristics, behavior, and habitat of the beaver.
ISBN: 1-56763-761-2 (hc)
1-56763-762-0 (pbk)
1. Beavers—Juvenile fiction. [1. Beavers—Fiction.] I. Sargent, Pat, 1936- II. Huff, Jeane Lirley, 1946- ill. III. Title. IV. Series: Sargent, Dave, 1941- Animal pride series ; 2.
PZ10.3.S243Bic 2003
[Fic]—dc21 96-001493

Factual information excerpted/adapted from THE WORLD BOOK ENCYCLOPEDIA.

Printed in the United States of America

Inspired by

our love of animals and the great outdoors and a desire to share our feelings with others.

Dedicated to

our special friend, James Rowe.

Foreword

Billy Beaver is shocked when his mother tells him that it is time for him to leave home and fend for himself. He soon finds himself alone in the woods. Scared but brave, young Billy struggles to conquer his fears.

Contents

If you would like to have the authors of the Animal Pride Series visit your school, free of charge, call 1-800-321-5671 or 1-800-960-3876.

One

Billy Leaves Home

It was a warm summer morning when Billy woke from a deep sleep. He lay on his bed and stretched and yawned, then rubbed his eyes, trying to wake up. After several minutes, he was fully awake.

Billy made his way to the lodge entrance and swam through the door. When he reached the surface of the pond, he could feel the warm rays from the morning sun hitting his head. After swimming for four or five minutes, Billy decided it was time to eat. He swam to the shore and made his way to the trees. And because he wasn't sure about what kind of bark he wanted for breakfast, he began tasting every tree. He came to a big sycamore that had tender bark and a sweet taste that he liked. He ate his fill of sycamore bark.

Billy went back to the pond to play *Catch Me If You Can* with the fish and the frogs.

The water was crystal clear, and it was easy for Billy Beaver to spot his friend, Joe Frog. Billy started chasing Joe Frog. Joe could turn fast in the water and hide under a small rock, and he did just that.

Billy Beaver swam back and forth several times trying to find Joe. Joe was lying under a rock, watching Billy, when Sally Catfish came swimming by. Sally Catfish loved to play with Billy Beaver and Joe Frog. She swam over to Billy, and Joe swam from his hiding place so they could play together.

The three of them swam around the pond for a long time before tiring out.

They all agreed it was time for a short nap. Then they would meet later in the afternoon.

Billy Beaver swam back to the lodge and lay on his bed. He was soon fast asleep. Sometime later he was awakened by a lot of chattering. His mom and dad were talking.

Billy heard his dad ask his mom, "Did you tell Billy what I told you to tell him?"

"No," Billy's mom replied, "I'm going to tell him as soon as he wakes up from his nap."

Billy's dad said, "I think I'll take a short nap now. I hope the wind dics down so I can chew down that elm tree near the dam. There are two good limbs on that tree that I need to finish the repairs on the dam. Then maybe those pesky raccoons won't be able to tear up the dam anymore." Billy's dad stretched out on his bed and went to sleep.

A few minutes later, Billy got up and started to leave the lodge. He heard his mom call, “Billy, I need to talk to you. Please meet me by the willow tree. I’ll be there as soon as I finish cleaning the floor.”

Billy Beaver waited patiently under the willow tree for his mother. When she got there, she sat down beside him and said, “Billy, it’s time for you to leave the lodge and the pond. You are grown now, and you must find a stream of your own where you can build a dam and a lodge for yourself. In time, you will find yourself a nice girlfriend. Your father has taught you all you need to know about building a dam and a lodge. I am your mother, and I’ll always love you, but the time has come for you to go, and nothing can change that. So, go now, Billy, and God bless you."

Billy watched his mother swim back toward the lodge. He lay there on the bank with his head resting on his front feet. Large tears fell from his eyes.

Billy said, "Where can I go? All my friends are here."

Realizing that he was no longer welcome and that he couldn't stay, Billy Beaver said, "Bye, Joe Frog. Bye, Sally Catfish. Bye, Mama and Daddy. I love you." He turned and slowly headed toward the mountains to find a stream of his own.

Two

Alone In The Woods

As Billy made his way up the mountainside, he found the traveling slow and tiring. His poor feet were getting sore from walking on rocks. He had never been on land for more than a few minutes at a time.

Billy was very hungry, and, realizing that it would soon be dark, decided to find a tree with a good-tasting bark for his dinner. And after he finished eating, he would be able to use a lot of the wood shavings for his bed.

For the first time in his life, he would be forced to sleep in the open. He would not have the comfort and security of the lodge.

As darkness drew near, Billy became frightened. He heard sounds of wild animals that he had never heard before. Timber wolves and coyotes were howling, and he heard the owls' "Whooo-Whooo".

Billy Beaver lay there quiet and still, listening to the new sounds. And with every new sound, his heart beat faster. He knew that there was no way he could sleep. He hoped the sun would soon come up.

The night passed slowly. From time to time, Billy heard the distant scream of a mountain lion. Then he heard leaves and brush rattling. The sound kept coming closer and closer.

The moon was now high in the sky, but the tall trees wouldn't let enough light shine through for him to see what was coming. The sounds grew nearer and nearer.

Billy Beaver was now in a panic, for whatever was coming was now only a few yards away, and his only defense was his sharp teeth.

Suddenly, a voice asked, “What are you doing here, Billy Beaver?”

To Billy Beaver's surprise, he saw Jack Moose standing there. He had seen Jack Moose drink from the beaver pond many times.

Billy said, "I was sent away to find a home of my own. I am no longer welcome at the pond or the lodge."

Jack Moose said, "I guess that means you are grown now, Billy."

Billy said, "I guess so. What are you doing here, Jack Moose?"

"I'm looking for a good warm place to lie down where I can spend the rest of the night," Jack replied.

"Why don't you spend the rest of the night here, Jack?" Billy asked. "I'll help you keep warm."

Knowing how scared Billy was, Jack Moose sai[illegible]ess this is as good a place as an[illegible]

Jack lay down beside Billy. Billy Beaver snuggled up close to Jack Moose. They both fell asleep.

The next morning at first light, Billy Beaver woke up to find that Jack Moose had already left.

Billy was hungry, so he started searching for some tender bark to eat. He finally found some. It wasn't his favorite, but it would have to do.

After eating his fill, Billy made his way to the top of the mountain. Once on top, Billy Beaver could see everywhere. He could see for miles in every direction.

Billy looked into the valley on the other side of the mountain and saw a small stream flowing gently through the valley. He thought it might make a good place for a pond. He ran as fast as he could down the mountainside. Once he reached the stream, he sat and looked for a long time, studying the lay of the land and the speed of the water. He knew that these things were very important when building a dam.

Billy checked all the trees, to be sure there would be enough growing near the stream to build a dam for the pond and a lodge to live in.

Once Billy was satisfied that everything he needed was there, he cut down a small tree with his sharp teeth and pulled it to the middle of the stream, where he started building a dam.

Three

Billy Finds a Wife

Billy Beaver worked hard on the dam every day. He cut down all the trees near the stream first and then cut them into pieces just so-so to build the dam.

Every day the dam was a little larger. And before long, Billy had a small pond. It wasn't very big at first, but it was the right size to swim around in.

After a few more days, the dam had backed the water up to the place where Billy Beaver wanted to build his lodge. Now, he would have to work on the dam part of the time, and part of the time would be spent on the lodge.

As Billy laid the first limbs to start the lodge, a big smile covered his face. He knew it wouldn't be much longer until he would have a nice, warm place to live. He also knew that when winter came, he couldn't survive without a lodge.

Billy worked hard and fast because he wanted to get his lodge finished. He was tired of sleeping in the open, and he was always afraid that a wild animal would attack him during the night.

Two more weeks passed before Billy had the dam tall enough so that water would back up all around his lodge. That night, for the first time in almost four months, Billy slept in the comfort and security of a lodge.

The next morning when Billy woke up, he left his lodge to find himself some breakfast. When he got outside, he noticed a chill in the air. It was much colder than usual, and everything was covered with frost. Billy knew that hard winter wasn't far off, and he still had a lot of work to do.

After eating a good breakfast, Billy went to work on the dam. He figured it would take about another month to finish it.

It was almost lunchtime before Billy stopped to rest and eat lunch. While he was eating, he saw another beaver coming toward the pond. Billy had worked hard on his pond, and he was not going to share it with anyone. As the beaver got closer, Billy Beaver showed his teeth and began beating his tail against the ground in anger. The beaver stopped and lay down. Billy could see that the beaver was crying.

Billy stopped displaying his anger. He could now see that the beaver was a girl. He walked up close and asked, “What’s wrong?”

She said, “I’m scared. I’m all alone, and I have no place to live.”

“Why don’t you build yourself a pond and a lodge?” Billy asked.

“Because I don’t know how,” she replied.

Billy thought for a minute or so, then asked, “What’s your name?”

“My name is Susie Beaver,” she replied in a soft voice, then asked, “What’s yours?”

“I’m Billy Beaver,” he stated proudly.

“You sure have a nice pond, Billy,” Susie said.

“Why, thanks,” Billy answered. “I like it, but I still have work to do.”

Susie said, “If you want, I could help you.”

Billy thought for a minute, then said, “I guess that will be all right.”

Billy and Susie started working together on the dam. They worked hard and fast.

Billy and Susie finished the dam just before hard winter set in. And it's a fact that, under beaver law, once beavers work together on a dam for their pond and lodge, they become husband and wife.

Billy and Susie lived happily ever after.

Four

Beaver Facts

A beaver is a furry animal with a wide flat tail that looks like a big paddle. Beavers are known for their skill at cutting down trees with their strong front teeth. They eat the bark and use the branches to build dams and lodges (homes) in the water. Beavers always seem to be working. That's why we call a hard-working person an "eager beaver" or say that person is as "busy as a beaver".

All beavers live in streams, rivers, and fresh-water lakes near woodlands. They are great divers and swimmers. A beaver can swim underwater for one-half mile and can hold its breath for fifteen minutes.

There are more beavers in the United States and Canada than anywhere else in the world. Beavers are also found in Asia and Europe.

The pioneers and Indians ate beaver meat and traded the furs for things they needed. In the late 1600s, a man could trade twelve beaver skins for a rifle. One beaver skin would buy four pounds of shot, or a kettle, or a pound of tobacco.

North American beavers are three to four feet long, including the tail, and weigh from forty to sixty pounds. Unlike most of the other mammals, beavers keep growing throughout their lives. Thousands of years ago, beavers of North America were about seven and a half feet long, including the tail—almost as long as the grizzly bears. No one knows why these huge beavers disappeared.

The beaver has a broad head with large and powerful jaws. Its rounded ears and small nostrils can close tightly to keep water out. A beaver has three eyelids on each eye. Two outer eyelids, one upper and one lower, fit around the eye. A transparent inner eyelid slides down over the eye and lets the animal see under water. On land, it protects the beaver's eye from sharp twigs when the beaver is cutting down trees. The beaver cannot see well, and it depends on its hearing and smell to warn it of danger.

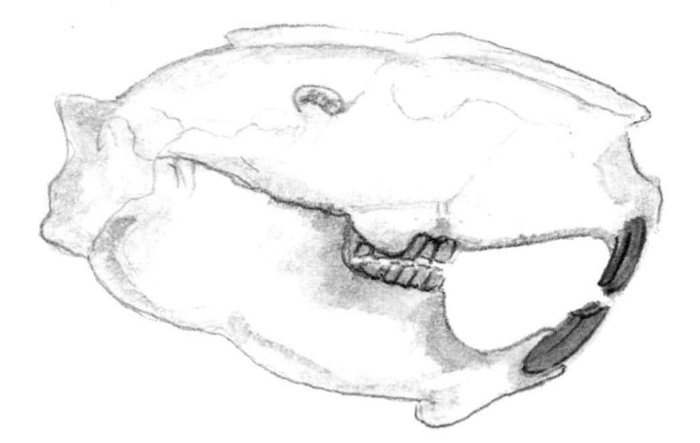

A beaver has twenty teeth: four strong curved front teeth for gnawing, and sixteen back teeth for chewing. The front teeth, called incisors, have a bright orange outer covering that is very hard. The back part of the incisors is much softer.

When a beaver gnaws, the back part of its incisors wears down much faster than the front part. As a result, these teeth have a very sharp chisel-like edge. The incisors never wear out because they keep growing throughout the animal's life. The back teeth have flat rough edges and stop growing when the beaver is about two years old.

The beaver's legs are short, and its feet are black. Tough skin, with little hairs, covers the feet. Each front paw ends in five toes that have long thick claws. A beaver has to use its long claws to dig up the roots of bushes and trees for food. When swimming, the animal usually makes tight fists of its front paws and holds them against its chest. Sometimes, when a beaver swims through underwater brush or grass, it uses its front paws to push the plants aside.

The back feet are larger than the front ones, and may be six to seven inches long. The toes are webbed and end in strong claws. Two claws on each foot are split. The beaver uses these splits to comb its fur. The webbed feet serve as flippers and help make the animal a powerful swimmer and diver.

The tail of a beaver is one of its most interesting features. The stiff flat tail looks like a paddle. It is about twelve inches long, six to seven inches wide, and three-fourths inch thick. A small part of the tail nearest the beaver's body has the same kind of fur as the body. The rest of the tail is covered with black scaly skin and has only a few stiff hairs. The beaver uses its tail to steer when it swims. The tail is also used as a prop when the animal stands on its hind legs to eat or to cut down trees. A beaver slaps its tail on the water to make a loud noise to warn other beavers of danger.

Beaver fur varies from shiny dark brown to yellowish brown. It looks black when wet. A beaver's coat has an underfur that helps keep the beaver comfortable in the water. This fur traps air and holds it close to the animal's skin. The trapped air acts as a protective blanket that keeps the beaver warm, even in icy water. The beaver's coat has long, heavy guard hairs that lie over the underfur and protect it.

Beavers live as long as twelve years. Their enemies include bears, lynxes, otters, wolverines, wolves, and man. A beaver avoids these enemies by living in the water and by coming out mostly at night to eat or work.

A female beaver carries her young inside her body for about three months before they are born. She has two to four babies at a time. Most young beavers, called kits or pups, are born in April or May. A newborn kit is about fifteen inches long, including its tail, and weighs one-half to one and one-half pounds. The tail is about three and a half inches long. A kit has soft fluffy fur at birth, and its eyes are open.

The young ones live with their parents for two years, and then are driven from the family group. These young adults are forced out to make room for the newborn. Beavers rarely fight with each other except in the spring, when the two-year-olds are driven away.

Beavers store food for winter use. They anchor branches and logs under the water near their lodges. In winter, they swim under the ice and eat the bark.

A beaver lodge looks somewhat like a tepee. The lodge may stand on the riverbank or in the water like an island. The tops of most lodges are three to six feet above the water. Holes between the branches in the ceiling let in fresh air. Each lodge has several underwater entrances and tunnels, all of which lead to an inside chamber. The floor is four to six inches above the water.

BEYOND "THE END" . . .

LANGUAGE LINKS

A beaver's diet consists of tasty bark, spicy roots, flavorful twigs, and delectable leaves—or so a beaver thinks! You are to think like a beaver for this adventure with our five senses. Explore each of the foods eaten by beavers using the five senses. Use your senses first, one at a time, and then your pencil.

With each food, concentrate. Block out other thoughts. Remember you are a beaver. Describe how each food looks, how it feels, how it smells, how it taste, and how it sounds when you bite into it!

Make a chart like this and write seeing words in the Sight column for that food, feeling words in the Touch column, etc. It might be helpful to make a list of seeing words, feeling words, smelling words, tasting words, and hearing words before you begin the chart. Your reward will be a basket of poplar tree bark!

FOOD	SIGHT	TOUCH
Bark		
Roots		
Twigs		
Leaves		

SMELL	TASTE	SOUND

CURRICULUM CONNECTIONS

The back part of a beaver's two front teeth wear away more rapidly than the front, leaving a sharp enameled chisel edge. This enables the beaver to cut down large trees, as large as 30 inches in diameter. Our teeth are not made to cut down trees, but they are very important to us. We must learn to take good care of them. Did you know the enamel on our teeth, the part that protects the tooth from the wear and tear of chewing, is the hardest substance in our body? What rules do you follow to keep your teeth healthy? Check out the American Dental Association's web site where you can learn about proper brushing and flossing and about healthy snacks. There are also puzzles and games! Go to <www.ada.org/public/topics/kids/index/html>.

Beavers have special adaptations to help them get along, like their flat, hard and scaly tail acts as a rudder while swimming and also helps them balance when cutting down a tree. Beavers also have webbed feet to help them swim. Humans have adaptations too. To test one of your adaptations, try buttoning your shirt without using your thumbs! Think about other adaptations of humans.

Beavers build dams by felling trees. A beaver can fell a 5-inch diameter tree in about 25 minutes and a 3-inch diameter tree in 10 minutes. How many 3-inch trees can a beaver fell in 1 hour?

THE ARTS

A beaver's lodge looks like a stick igloo. He builds it with sticks, grass, and moss, woven together and plastered with mud.

Can you build a miniature beaver lodge in an aluminum pie pan?

THE BEST I CAN BE

The beaver is said to have the mind of an expert engineer. It is a hard-working animal. That's where the term "eager beaver" came from. Determine to be an eager beaver in your family, willingly doing your share of chores and actions to make your family comfortable and happy.